MARGRET & H. A. REY'S

Curious George

Plays Soccer

Written by Monica Perez

Illustrated in the style of H. A. Rey by Anna Grossnickle Hines

Houghton Mifflin Harcourt

Boston   New York

www.hmhco.com

The text type was set in Garamond.

ISBN 978-0-544-91246-5
Manufactured in China
SCP 10 9 8 7 6 5 4 3 2 1
4500639500

George is a good little monkey and always very curious.
He was at the park on this beautiful day, ready to play.

But where were all of George's friends? Not at the fountain or the playground. Oh—everyone was at the field!

George watched for a moment. His good friend Gracie was there. The children were playing a game with a ball and a big net. George wanted to play too!

As soon as the ball passed near him, George ran after it. He ducked under a player's leg and grabbed the ball. Then he threw it into the nearby net. It made it in! George jumped in excitement.

But no one else was excited. "George," Gracie said, shaking her head. "Soccer has rules! The most important one is that you can't touch the ball with your hands if you're not the goalie."

George watched the rest of the game from a bench.
When it was over, Gracie and the coach came by.
"I'm Coach Sandy," the woman said. "Why don't you come
to soccer camp at the rec center? It starts tomorrow. We'll
teach you everything you need to know to play soccer."

Hooray! It was lucky that George had to wait only one day. Then he could get as good as Gracie, who had scored two points for her team.

The man with the yellow hat dropped George off at the rec center the next morning with his own soccer ball and a water bottle. George waved to Gracie, who was lining up with some of the older players. George was ready to play, and this time he knew to kick the ball instead of throw.

But before they played a game, George's group practiced their skills. Coach Sandy called them drills. They dribbled around cones on the ground. George learned that dribbling is moving the ball with your feet. That was fun, but soon George became more interested in stacking the cones.

After snack, George and his teammates practiced kicking the ball back and forth with a partner. George thought he would try to balance the ball on his nose like a seal.

Finally, Coach Sandy announced, "Time for a game! We have ten players in our group, so each team gets five. One goalkeeper will defend the net. The other four players will pass the ball to each other and try to kick it into the net before the goalkeeper can stop it."

Coach Sandy handed out red pinnies to George's team. He put one on. George wanted to be goalie so he could touch the ball with his hands, but Mia played goalie this time. George was a striker.

George tried to make shots into the goal, but he wasn't very good at it. He kept kicking the ball too hard and too far. Every time this happened, the other team got to throw the ball back in. "It's okay. Just try again!" said the coach.

Whew, what a day! Every part of George was tired. He waved goodbye to his friend Gracie. He hoped he'd get better at soccer soon.

On Tuesday, it was George's turn to be a defender. His job was to keep the other team from getting the ball too close to the net. "Remember, George," Coach Sandy said. "Keep your eye on the ball!"

George knew he had to keep his eye on the ball, but it wasn't long before he got distracted by the butterflies.

Every day, George learned a little more about soccer. He tried very hard to be a team player. But sometimes little monkeys forget. Like the time he forgot he was supposed to deliver the pinnies to the next field and tried them all on instead.

Or the time he gathered some friends so they could launch their balls down the playground slide when they were supposed to be heading back to the field.

On the last day of the soccer camp, George was excited for the big game. Everyone was invited to play, and friends and family came to watch. George waved happily to the man with the yellow hat.

George was on the blue team. He cheered for his friends and waited patiently for his turn to play. Unfortunately, George's teammates were having a hard time defending their goal. The yellow team scored three times.

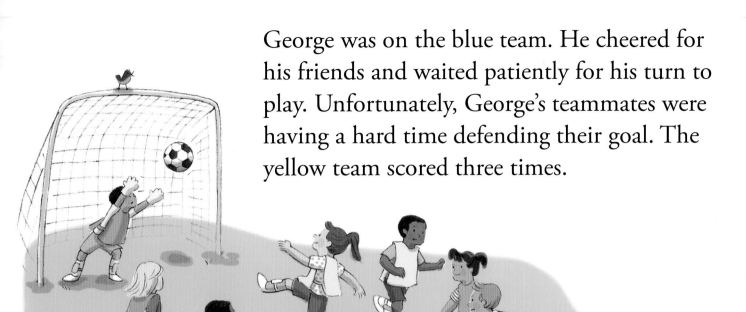

The blue team's goalie, Isaac, was ready for a break. The coach asked for a volunteer to replace him. George jumped as high as he could.

The coach chose him! George took up his position in front of the net. This time George didn't get distracted. And he didn't get bored. Instead, he played like only a monkey can, and he stopped goal after goal after goal.

The coach chose him! George took up his position in front of the net. This time George didn't get distracted. And he didn't get bored. Instead, he played like only a monkey can, and he stopped goal after goal after goal.

George was on the blue team. He cheered for his friends and waited patiently for his turn to play. Unfortunately, George's teammates were having a hard time defending their goal. The yellow team scored three times.

The blue team's goalie, Isaac, was ready for a break. The coach asked for a volunteer to replace him. George jumped as high as he could.

The final score was close. The yellow team won—three to two. But George was the blue team's hero of the day. He had stopped four goals!

"So, what do you think of soccer now?" Gracie asked George the next day at the park. George smiled and dribbled circles around her. Gracie laughed and said, "Now, that's talking with your feet!"